THE Spooky Wheels on the Bus

by J. Elizabeth Mills
illustrated by Ben Mantle

Cartwheel
·B·O·O·K·S·®

SCHOLASTIC INC.

New York   Toronto   London   Auckland   Sydney   Mexico City   New Delhi   Hong Kong

To Lia Mojica—
maker of cut-paper bats, cottony webs, monsters on the door, and all kinds of spooky treats…
Happy Halloween!
—J.E.M.

For Arwen
—B.M.

Text copyright © 2010 by J. Elizabeth Mills.
Illustrations copyright © 2010 by Scholastic Inc.
All rights reserved. Published by Scholastic Inc.
SCHOLASTIC, CARTWHEEL BOOKS, and associated logos are trademarks and/or registered trademarks of Scholastic Inc.

Library of Congress Cataloging-in-Publication Data is available.
ISBN 978-0-545-17480-0

28 27 26 25   17 18 19/0

Designed by Angela Jun
Printed in the U.S.A.   40
First printing, July 2010

One spooky bus goes **RATTLE** and **SHAKE**,
RATTLE and **SHAKE**, **RATTLE** and **SHAKE**.

One spooky bus goes **RATTLE** and **SHAKE**,
All through the town.

Two white wipers go CREAK, CREAK, CREAK,
CREAK, CREAK, CREAK. CREAK, CREAK, CREAK.

Two white wipers go **CREAK, CREAK, CREAK,**
All through the town.

Three noisy cats go **MEOW, HISS, HISS,
MEOW, HISS, HISS. MEOW, HISS, HISS.**

Three noisy cats go **MEOW, HISS, HISS,**
All through the town.

Four glowing wheels roll **ROUND** and **ROUND**,
ROUND and **ROUND**, **ROUND** and **ROUND**.

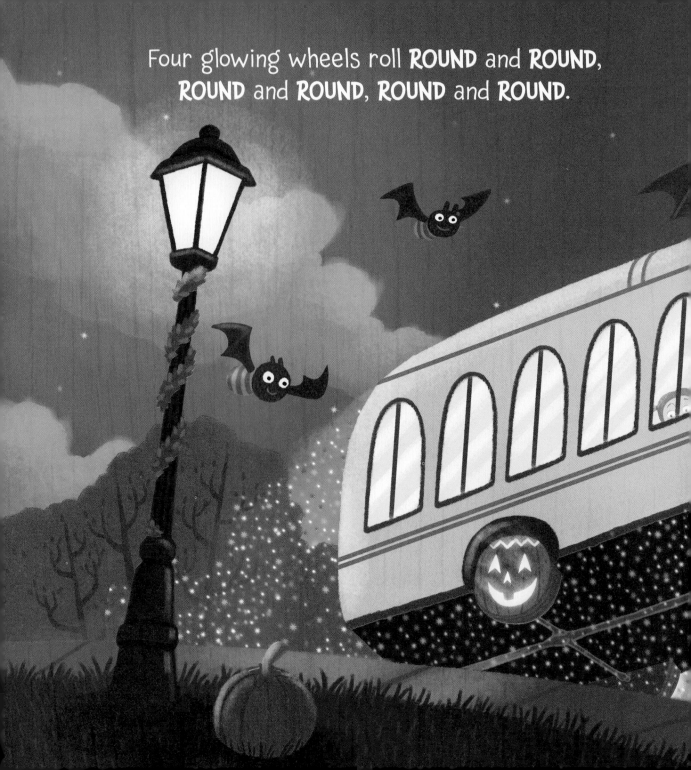

Four glowing wheels roll **ROUND** and **ROUND**,
All through the town.

Five big spiders **SPIN THEIR WEBS,**
SPIN THEIR WEBS, SPIN THEIR WEBS.

Five big spiders **SPIN THEIR WEBS**,
All through the town.

Six singing mummies HUM, HUM, HUM,
HUM, HUM, HUM. HUM, HUM, HUM.

Six singing mummies **HUM, HUM, HUM,**
All through the town.

Seven silly monsters **WIGGLE** and **WAGGLE**, **WIGGLE** and **WAGGLE**, **WIGGLE** and **WAGGLE**.

Seven silly monsters **WIGGLE** and **WAGGLE**,
All through the town.

Eight wacky witches **CACKLE** and **HOWL**,
CACKLE and **HOWL**, **CACKLE** and **HOWL**.

Eight wacky witches **CACKLE** and **HOWL**,
All through the town.

Nine magic brooms go **SWISH, SWOOSH, SWISH,**
SWISH, SWOOSH, SWISH. SWISH, SWOOSH, SWISH.

Nine magic brooms go **SWISH, SWOOSH, SWISH,**
All through the town.

Ten goofy ghosts say, "BOO-OO-OO, BOO-OO-OO, BOO-OO-OO."

Ten goofy ghosts say, "**BOO-OO-OO**,"
All through the town.

One spooky bus goes **RATTLE** and **SHAKE**,
RATTLE and **SHAKE**, **RATTLE** and **SHAKE**.

One spooky bus goes **RATTLE** and **SHAKE** . . .

On **Halloween** night!